WHATLEY'S QUEST

WRITTEN BY

Bruce Whatley & Rosie Smith

ILLUSTRATED BY

Bruce Whatley

HarperCollinsPublishers

For Mum whose love and perseverance gave me
the gift of my right arm. And for Dad ~a true craftsman.
Bruce

For Mum with love and in loving memory of Dad.
Rosie

For our children, Ben and Ellyn.
Thank you for your inspiration and patience.
May your aim be true.
Love from Mum and Dad

First published in 1994 in Australia by Angus & Robertson,
an imprint of HarperCollins Publishers, 25 Ryde Road,
Pymble, Sydney, NSW 2073, Australia.

Whatley's Quest
Copyright © 1994 by Bruce Whatley
Concept by Rosie Smith and Bruce Whatley
Printed in the U.S.A. All rights reserved.
1 2 3 4 5 6 7 8 9 10
❖
First American Edition, 1995
ISBN 0-06-026291-5
ISBN 0-06-026292-3 (lib. bdg.)

The arrow has been launched. . . . The Alphabet Quest is on!

As you embark on your journey through the twenty-six letters of the alphabet, you will be on a quest for buried treasure. All kinds of adventures await you, but you must look carefully; this book rewards only the sharp-eyed and curious. Are you ready to accept the challenge? Well, then . . . let's begin!

Here are a few clues to help you on your way:

❖*Look for the hidden letters on each page. Some are easy to find, and some are cleverly tucked away, so don't give up. Good things come to those who look and look!*

❖*Hunt for all the animals and objects beginning with the same letter on each page. How many can you find? Some of the words are listed on the endpapers, but you can find many, many more.*

❖*Make up sentences from the words you find. Gorilla is glum as he touches the globe with his glove; what about Pirate Pig? How many words beginning with the same letter can you use in a single sentence?*

❖*Make up stories out of your sentences and out of the words you find. Follow these stories through the pages. Is Gorilla glum because Fox has filched a fragment of his treasure map? What happens to Horse? The stories and illustrations are continuous, but only you can find the words to connect them!*

❖*Discover the treasure waiting for you at your journey's end. Knowledge is the key, and with this key you can unlock the secret of the letters and use their magic forever!*

mist❖alchemy❖algebra❖align❖allegory❖alopecia❖amazement❖amber❖amethyst❖amuse❖anchor❖ancient❖angle❖animal
nadillo❖armlet❖armor❖army❖arrow❖asparagus❖astray❖astrolabe❖astronomer❖astronomy❖attempt❖awe❖awesome❖axe
ison❖bite❖black❖blue❖blush❖blushing❖boat❖bob❖bold❖bolt❖bone❖book❖bounce❖bounced❖bow❖boy❖brass❖bronze❖
nel❖camlet❖camouflage❖canary❖candelabra❖candle❖candlestick❖canister❖cape❖carrying❖carved❖

checkered❖cheese❖chef❖chest❖chestnut❖chimpanzee❖chipmunk❖chirp❖choice❖chortle❖chuckle❖cuticle❖clairvoyant❖claw
crab❖crack❖crazy❖crescent❖crest❖crimson❖crocodile❖cross❖crossbow❖crown❖crystal ball❖curls❖curly❖cushion
am❖dial❖diamond❖diaphanous❖dinner❖dinosaur❖dish❖dismay❖dividers❖dodo❖dome❖dome-headed❖dominoes❖donkey
dupe❖eagle❖ear❖earring❖earth❖east❖eat❖eccentric❖eclipse❖edge❖egg❖eggcup❖eggshell❖Egyptian❖eight❖elaborate❖
epaulet❖equator❖equinox❖err❖escape❖espadrilles❖exasperated❖exotic❖expedition❖exploration❖expression❖eye❖eyeball
ellow❖felt❖fence❖fez❖fin❖find❖finger❖fingernail❖fire❖fish❖fishing basket❖fishing line❖fishing rod❖fist❖five❖five-o'clock
florid❖flower❖fluffy❖flute❖fluttering❖flying❖folded❖folds❖follow❖foot❖footslogger❖force❖forearm❖forefinger❖forehead
full❖fulvous❖fur❖fusilier❖gabble❖gaggle❖gamekeeper❖gander❖gargantuan❖garment❖garnet❖garnish❖gash❖gate❖gauntlet
ler❖globe❖glove❖glum❖goanna❖goat❖go-between❖goblet❖goggles❖going❖gold❖golden egg❖goldfish❖gong❖goose❖gorilla
scope❖hair❖halter❖hamster❖hand❖handkerchief❖handle❖hank❖happy❖harangue❖hare❖harp❖hat❖haversack❖hawking❖hawser
us❖hive❖hoe❖hoist❖holding❖hole❖holler❖honeycomb❖honk❖hood❖hoof❖hook❖hoop❖hop❖horn❖horrified❖horse❖horseshoe
mplement❖impossible❖imprison❖in❖Indian❖indigo❖individual❖inertia❖ingenious❖ingot❖initial❖ink❖innocent❖inscription❖
packed❖jape❖japer❖jar❖jaw❖jester❖jewel❖jewelry❖jigsaw❖jocose❖jocund❖jolly❖journey❖joust❖joyful❖jug❖juggle❖jute❖
kiltie❖kind❖kindling❖king❖kingfisher❖kink❖kirtle❖kith❖kiwi❖knapsack❖knave❖knee❖knight❖knit❖knob❖knot❖knuckle
dybird❖lag❖lamb❖lambent❖lament❖lamp❖lance❖lantern❖lap❖lapel❖lappet❖large❖lariat❖lashings❖lasso❖last❖latch❖latitude
lettering❖lever❖lid❖liege❖light❖lighthouse❖lightning❖lilac❖lime❖limn❖line❖linear❖link❖linkwork❖lion❖lip❖list❖little❖
lurch❖luxuriant❖mace❖magenta❖magnet❖magnify❖magnifying glass❖magpie❖mail❖male❖mallet❖mammals❖mammoth❖
suring tape❖medal❖medley of maps❖meeting❖melon❖memorable❖mend❖merciful❖message❖message in a bottle❖messy❖
moving❖music❖nab❖nail❖Napoleon Mouse❖Napoleonic❖narwhal❖nascent❖naught❖naughty❖near❖nebulous❖needle❖nest❖
number❖nurse❖nurture❖oar❖oarsman❖oasis❖obelisk❖obfuscation❖object❖objects❖obligation❖oblique❖oblong❖obnoxious❖
off-white❖ogle❖ogling❖oh❖old❖old-world❖olive❖one❖onions❖oops❖openmouthed❖opposition❖opt❖orange❖orangutan❖orb
adlock❖pail❖paint❖paintbrush❖pair❖paisley❖paletot❖pallor❖palm❖palm frond❖pan❖panda❖panel❖panic❖pantograph❖pants
uliar❖peep❖peer❖peg leg❖pelage❖pelican❖penalty❖pendant❖penguin❖penna❖pennant❖pennon❖perched❖peregrination❖peril
s❖pinion❖pink❖pinnacle❖piping❖pirate❖piscivorous pelican❖pitchfork❖plank❖pleat❖plight❖plug❖plumage❖plumate❖plumb
precarious❖preparation❖presiding❖prickly❖proboscis❖prod❖protest❖prow❖pull❖pumpkin❖punish❖punishment❖pupil❖puppet
uality❖qualms❖quandary❖quarrel❖quarry❖quarter❖quartet❖quartz❖quaver❖quay❖queen❖quell❖querulous❖query❖quest❖
n marks❖quotes❖rabbit❖rabble-rouser❖raccoon❖race❖racketeer❖radiating❖raft❖rag❖ragged❖raggedy❖rags❖raiment❖rain❖
realm❖rear❖rebus❖reckless❖rectangle❖red❖red ribbon❖reed❖reef knot❖regal❖relic❖relief map❖relief motif❖remarkable❖
rising sun❖rivage❖river❖rivets❖rock❖rocking❖rodent❖rogue❖rope❖rose❖round table❖row❖rowing❖royal blue❖rubiginous
fe❖safeguard❖sagging❖sagittal❖sail❖sailor❖salient❖sallet❖sally forth❖saltire❖salute❖sand❖sandal❖sapphire❖sash❖saucepan
rewdriver❖scroll❖scrutiny❖scutcheon❖sea❖seaborne❖seafaring❖seagull❖seal❖seaman❖search❖seat❖see❖seeking❖selachian❖
lder❖shovel❖shroud❖sideburns❖sight❖signal❖silly❖sinister❖sinking sailor❖sinking ship❖sisal❖sitting❖six❖skating❖skunk❖
ner❖spider❖spindrift❖spiral❖splash❖spots❖spray❖squall❖squares❖staircase❖stalwart❖stand❖stars❖stash❖staves❖steadfast❖
washbuckling❖swinging❖sword❖symbol❖tablecloth❖tache❖taciturn❖tail❖talisman❖talons❖tame❖tan❖tankard❖target❖tartan
thrilling❖through❖thumb❖tick❖tied❖tiger❖tight❖tigress❖tin❖tip❖toad❖toadstool❖toby jug❖toe❖toe cap❖toggle❖tongue❖
re❖triangle❖tricky❖trumpet❖trumpeting❖tubular❖tulip❖tunic❖turkey❖turquoise❖twelve❖twenty❖twined❖twins❖twisted❖
nts❖undertaking❖underwear❖undone❖undulating❖uneven❖unfastened❖unfortunate❖unhappy❖unhook❖unicorn❖uniform❖
egetable❖veil❖vent❖vermilion❖vertex❖vertical❖vertices❖vertigo❖vessel❖vest❖vested❖veteran❖vex❖viaduct❖vicinage❖
e❖voyage❖vulture❖waders❖waist❖waistband❖waistcoat❖waistline❖waiting❖wale❖walk❖walking❖walkway❖wall-eyed
rks❖wave❖waver❖way❖wayfarer❖wayfaring❖wayward❖wealth❖wear and tear❖wearing❖weary❖weasel❖weathered❖
tley❖wheat❖wheel❖wheelbarrow❖whet❖whim❖whimsical❖whiskers❖white❖wick❖wicker basket❖wickerwork
wonderment❖wonderstruck❖wood❖woodborer❖wooden❖woof❖words❖working❖worm❖worthy❖wound❖woven
zebra❖zenith❖zeroed in❖zestful❖zig-zag❖zinnia❖zircon❖zodiac❖and many many more words for you to find❖

Archer, draw back your bow
for you will direct our journey.

Our Quest~
the pursuit of knowledge
and the gathering of wisdom.

Archer, aim your arrow high,
and may your aim be true.

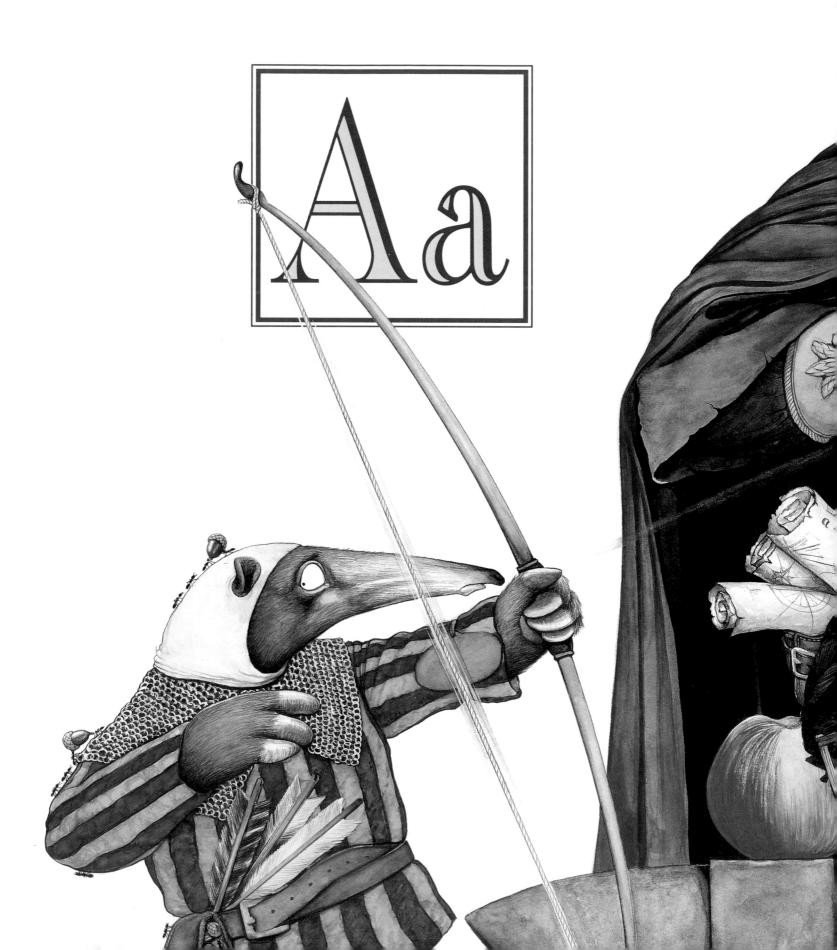

Bb

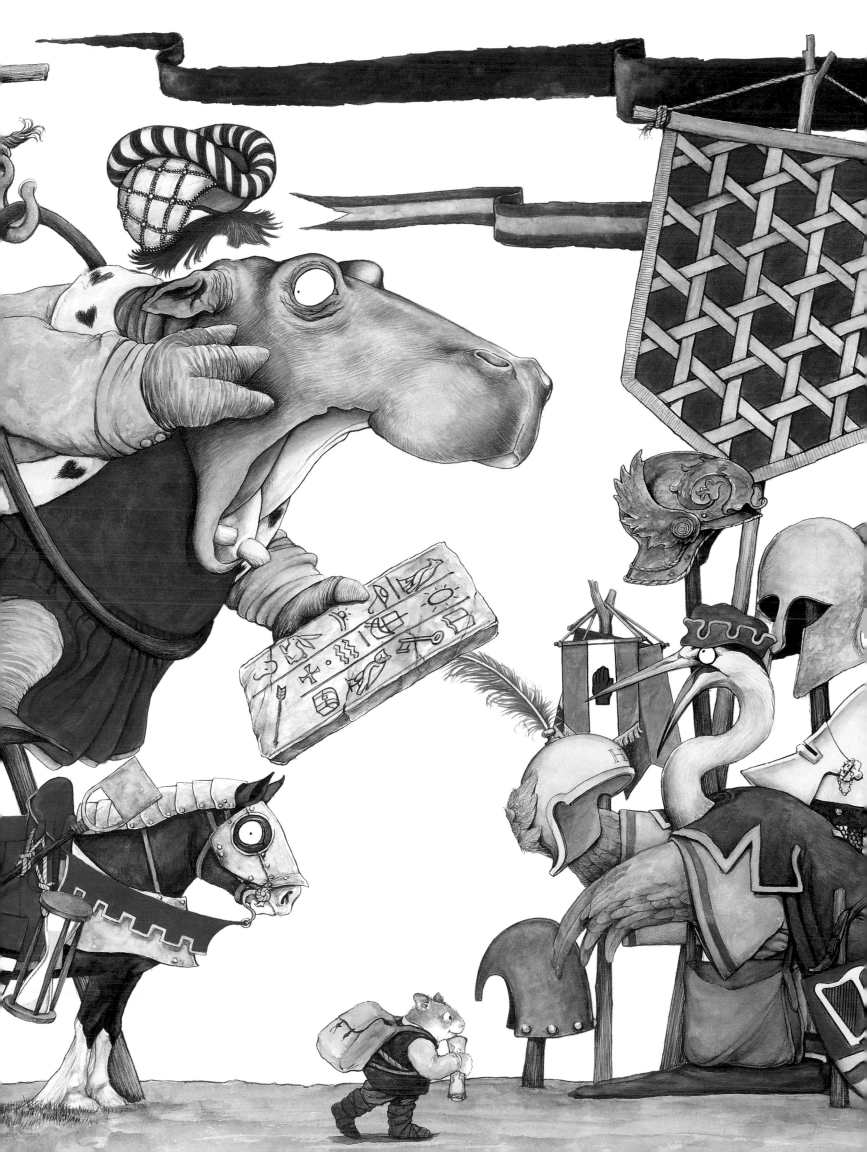

Mm
Nn

Oo

Pp

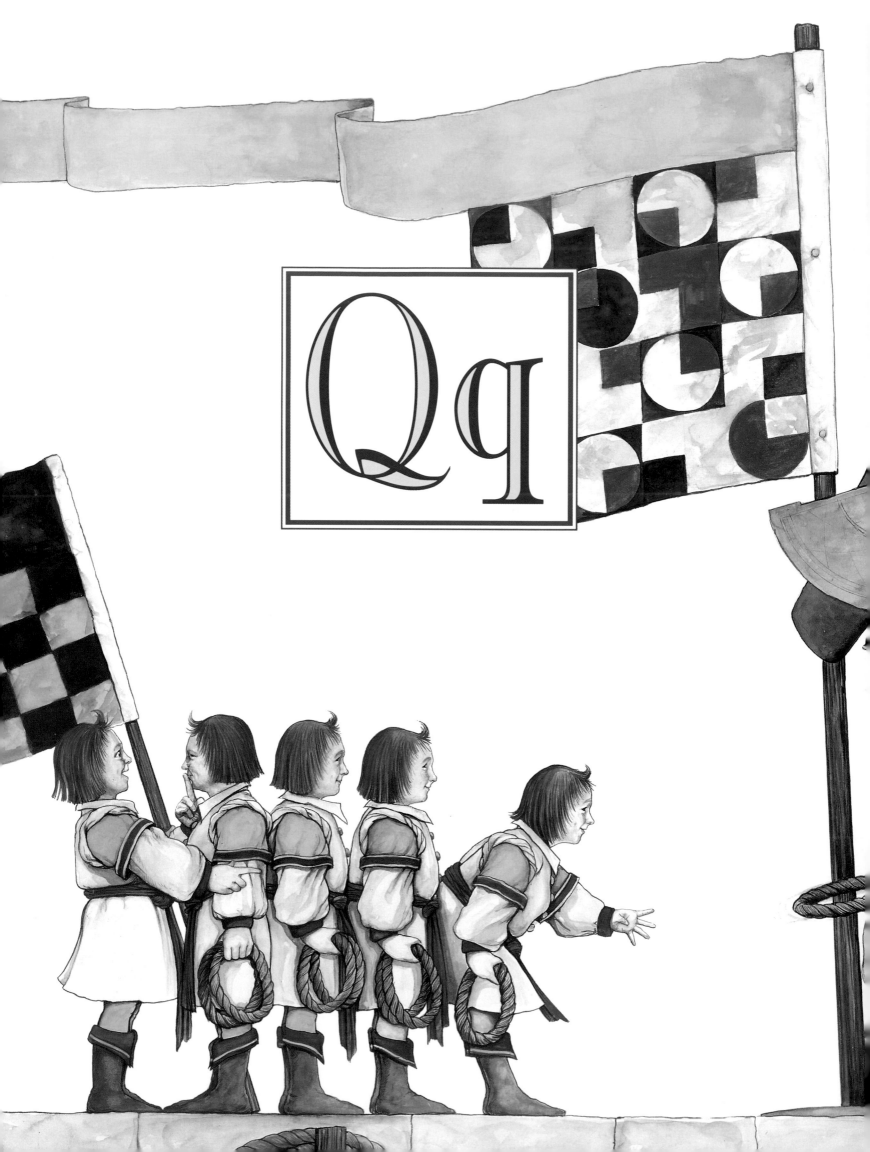

Uu
Vv

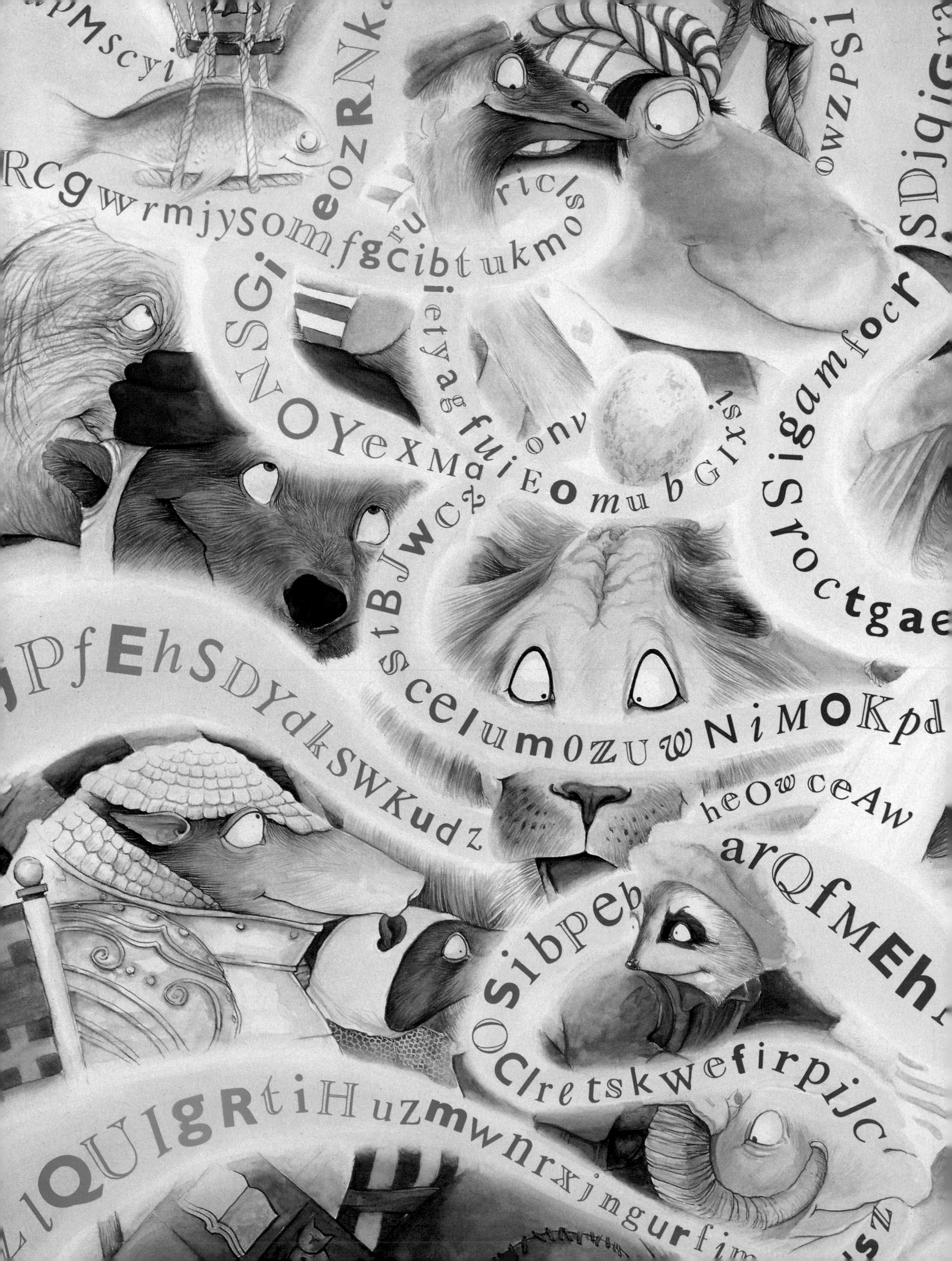

Now it is your Quest…
Always aim your arrow high,
and may your aim be true.

igtkfsBnuiopKnowledgerbcKeyxehcMhiadfvc

uigktreasurejsaDiscoveryHZyujomJoyasDGk

oewiehtgrlnjourneyLbxcuqfawpvsdrftkjiufloenb

ixaroNwrpsuveaimbervtrueqotbizyujmaxmef

ucarfgtvlnwisdomtLbxcuqfawpvsdrftkjiufloenbvfgt

hyselBOwrnevsypoglexvtiArrowghbwtnkcsaft

qrvluawisdomwHjntriumphiBeOthujdbtoivl

maRfgtvlndiscoveRyxcuqfawpjOyrftkjiufloenbvf

fipnadzvxokqehtgrlnjourneyLbxcuqfawp

wyrabuCasnevpevabhlaxybEjfpnbvdntgat

eoseloAiCnbuieyhlervtiAlbeavwtocsziesabdvud

sdRfbaxnASRntruewyhlervtiKnowledgecug

abacus❖ability❖able❖above❖accident❖accountant❖accurate❖achieve❖acorn❖action❖add❖adversary❖advise❖aim❖albatross❖
❖annoying❖answer❖ant❖antagonist❖anteater❖antique❖ants❖anvil❖anxious❖apple❖appliqué❖arc❖archer❖ardent❖arr
❖back❖bag❖ball❖banana❖banner❖baseball❖baseball glove❖basket❖bat❖beak❖bear❖behind❖bell❖belt❖beret❖big❖bill❖b
brooding❖brown❖brown bear❖buffalo❖bull❖bullock❖bunting❖burly❖butterfly❖button❖buttonhole❖cage❖call❖callin
castellations❖castle❖caterpillar❖Celtic cross❖chain❖chair❖challenge❖chameleon❖champion❖character❖chartreuse❖charts❖
❖cloak❖cloudy❖cob❖cobweb❖collar❖column❖comet❖compass❖cone❖consult❖cook❖cord❖core❖corn❖corner❖coupe❖co
❖dagger❖dais❖dame❖damsel❖danger❖day❖dazed❖dead❖decoy❖deduce❖deer❖defiant❖demand❖design❖device❖diagonal❖
❖dot❖doubtful❖down❖dozen❖dragon❖drake❖drape❖drawing❖dreadful❖dreaming❖drill❖drink❖drop❖drum❖drumstick❖
elbow❖elegant❖elephant❖eleven❖elf❖embarrass❖emblem❖emerald❖empty❖emu❖encounter❖end❖ensign❖enterprise❖en
❖eyeballing❖eyeful❖eyesight❖fable❖fabric❖face❖facial❖faithful❖falcon❖falling❖fans❖fast❖fastening❖fat❖fawning❖feather❖
shadow❖fixated❖flag❖flag bearer❖flageolet❖flagman❖flags❖flagstone❖flame❖flat❖fletching❖flight❖flights❖floating❖floc
❖foresight❖fork❖forward❖foul deed❖four❖fowl❖fox❖fragile❖fragment❖frayed❖freckles❖free❖friend❖frill❖fringe❖frog❖fr
❖gawking❖gazing❖geese❖gem❖gentle❖geography❖gesture❖giant❖gift❖gigantic❖girdle❖girl❖girth❖give❖glance❖glaucou
❖gosh❖granny❖grapes❖grass❖grasshopper❖grate❖gray❖green❖grill❖grim❖grimace❖grip❖grooves❖ground❖guide❖guinea pig
❖hear❖hearts❖heavy❖helmet❖helping❖hen❖henna❖heraldry❖heron❖hexagon❖hiding❖hieroglyphics❖hiking❖hill❖hinge❖hippo
❖hourglass❖ibex❖ibis❖iceberg❖icon❖ideograph❖igloo❖iguana❖illustration❖image❖imago❖immure❖impact❖imperfect❖imp
insect❖inset❖inside❖intent❖intersect❖intricate❖intrigue❖involute❖iris❖irons❖irregular❖island❖italic❖ivy❖jack❖jacket❖jade
kaleidoscope❖kangaroo❖kayak❖keel❖keep❖keg❖kern❖kettle❖kettledrum❖key❖keyhole❖key ring❖keystone❖khaki❖kick❖ki
❖koala❖koan❖kudos❖label❖labor❖labyrinth❖lace❖lacerated❖laces❖lacing❖lackadaisical❖lacuna❖lad❖ladder❖laden❖ladle❖la
❖lattice❖laugh❖lavender❖laying❖leaf❖lean❖leaping❖learn❖leather❖ledge❖left❖leg❖leggings❖lemon❖length❖lens❖leopard❖
lively❖lizard❖load❖loaded❖lobster❖lock❖locket❖locks❖locus❖lolling❖long❖longitude❖look❖loop❖lounging❖love❖lucky❖
mandarin❖mango❖manhandle❖map❖maple leaf❖marble❖maroon❖mascot❖massif❖mast❖mastodon❖mauve❖maze❖measure
metal❖metric❖milestone❖military❖mitten❖mole❖moleskins❖monocle❖moon❖moose❖motif❖mound❖mountain❖mouse❖m
net❖nightdress❖nightgown❖nightingale❖nine❖ninety❖noble❖nook❖noose❖north❖nose❖nostril❖notation❖notches❖notebook❖
observe❖obstacle❖obstruct❖obverse❖obvious❖occupant❖occurrence❖ocher❖ochroid❖octagon❖octant❖octopod❖octopus❖odd
❖ordeal❖ordinary❖orifice❖origami❖orle❖ornery❖ostrich❖outwit❖oval❖overbearing❖overcome❖ovoid❖owl❖pace❖pack❖pad
❖paper❖parallel❖parcel❖parchment❖parody❖parrot❖part❖passenger❖passing❖patch❖patchwork❖paunch❖paw❖pawn❖pearls
❖periphery❖perplexed❖personnel❖persuade❖pettitoes❖pewter❖pi❖pick❖pickax❖pied❖pier❖pig❖piglet❖pigtail❖pillars❖pine
❖plumb bob❖plumb line❖plummet❖plumose❖plunder❖plunger❖pocket❖point❖poke❖pole❖polka dots❖porky❖port❖pose
❖puppy❖purple❖purposeful❖push❖quad❖quadrangle❖quadrant❖quadrate❖quadrilateral❖quadruped❖quadruplet❖quail❖qua
question mark❖queue❖quibble❖quiet❖quiff❖quill❖quilt❖quilted map❖quintain❖quintuplet❖quiver❖quizzical❖quoits❖qu
rainbow❖rainproof❖rake❖ram❖ramification❖rampart❖rapids❖rapt❖rascal❖rash❖rasp❖ratiné❖ratline❖rattle❖ray❖reaction❖re
repair❖repine❖resting❖retard❖reverberate❖rhinoceros❖rhombus❖riant❖ribbon❖ricochet❖ridiculous❖rigging❖right❖ring❖ri
❖ruby❖rucksack❖rudder❖ruin❖ruminant❖rump❖rung❖running❖rush❖rushes❖russet❖rust❖sable❖sack❖sad❖saddle❖sad sac
❖save❖saw❖sawfish❖scabbard❖scalawag❖scan❖scarf❖scarlet❖scatterbrain❖scheming❖science❖scissors❖scoop❖screen❖scre
semaphore❖semicircle❖sentient❖serpent❖set of sails❖seven❖sextant❖shark❖sharp❖shells❖shelter❖shield❖ship❖shirt❖shoe
sky❖sleeve❖slipping❖slow❖sly❖smell❖smile❖snake❖snout❖snow❖snow leopard❖snow cloud❖sock❖sortie❖south❖spade
steeve❖stench❖stern❖stink❖stitches❖stitching❖store❖stouthearted❖stow❖straps❖stubble❖stud❖sun❖surf❖surfing❖survey❖s
❖task❖tassel❖taunt❖taut❖team❖teapot❖tear❖teasing❖telescope❖ten❖tethered❖texture❖thimble❖thistle❖thorn❖thorny❖threat
toot❖torch❖torn❖torque❖tortoise❖toucan❖tourists❖tow❖toward❖towards❖tower❖towrope❖trail❖transit❖travelers❖traveling
two❖umbrage❖umbrella❖unbearable❖unbolt❖unbuttoned❖unceremonious❖uncork❖uncovered❖under❖underarm❖underline❖ur
united❖unlock❖unlucky❖unruffled❖up❖uphold❖uplift❖upon❖upset❖upside-down❖upstream❖upturn❖valiant❖valley❖varied❖
vicinity❖Viking❖vim❖vincible❖vine❖viola❖violate❖violence❖violet❖violin❖virtuous❖vitality❖vixen❖volant❖volcano❖volitant
❖walnut❖walrus❖wandering❖want❖ward❖warm-hearted❖warp❖watch❖watching❖water❖waterborne❖waterfall❖watering can❖wa
web❖wee❖weft❖weight❖weighty❖well❖well-balanced❖well-being❖wending❖west❖westering❖westwards❖wet❖whale❖wharf
❖wide❖will❖willing❖willy-nilly❖wily❖wind❖windmill❖winsome❖wise❖wishbone❖wisp❖wizard❖woebegone❖wolf❖wombat❖w
❖wrinkles❖wrist❖writing❖xeric❖x-ray fish❖xylophone❖yacht❖yak❖yap❖yapok❖yarn❖yellow❖yes❖yoke❖youthful❖zany❖zea